ZOOMERANG ►a◄ BOOMERANG

POEMS

TO MAKE YOUR BELLY LAUGH

Compiled by Caroline Parry

Illustrated by Michael Martchenko

PUFFIN BOOKS

Acknowledgements

For each of the selections listed below, grateful acknowledgement is made
for permission to reprint original or copyrighted material, as follows:

"Hello, hello": From *You Be Good & I'll Be Night* by Eve Merriam. A Morrow Junior Book. Copyright © 1988 by Eve Merriam. All Rights Reserved. Reprinted by permission of Marian Reiner for the author.

Zoomerang a Boomerang: book title and poem © 1987, Ruth I. Dowell, used with permission of Gryphon House, Inc., Mt. Rainier, MD. USA.

Skyscraper: "Skyscraper" by Dennis Lee from *Alligator Pie* by Dennis Lee, published by Macmillan of Canada, © 1974, Dennis Lee.

Garbage Day: "Garbage Day" from *Toes in My Nose* by Sheree Fitch. Copyright © 1987 by Sheree Fitch. Published by Doubleday Canada Ltd. Reprinted by permission of Doubleday Canada Ltd.

Oh My, No More Pie: Words and music by Ella Jenkins, member of ASCAP. Ellbern Publishing, 1844 North Mohawk St., Chicago, Illinois 60614.

Everything Grows: Words and music by Raffi, D. Pike. © 1987 Homeland Publishing, a division of Troubadour Records Ltd. Used by Permission. From the album *Everything Grows* (Raffi).

Winter Signs: "Winter Signs" from *It's Snowing, It's Snowing* by Jack Prelutsky. Text © 1984 by Jack Prelutsky. Greenwillow Books, New York. Used by permission of William Morrow and Company, Inc./Publishers, New York. Appears here by arrangement with Houghton Mifflin Canada Limited under special license approved by the original publishers.

Jamboree: "Jamboree" from *All Day Long* by David McCord. Copyright © 1965, 1966 by David McCord. By permission of Little, Brown and Company.

another poem: From *Well, you can imagine*, by sean o huigin © 1983, by permission of sean o huigin and Black Moss Press.

Tooth Day: "Tooth Day" by Beatrice Schenk de Regniers; from *A Bunch of Poems and Verses*, © 1977 by Beatrice Schenk de Regniers, permission of the author.

Everywhere: From *Giants, Moosequakes & Other Disasters*, © 1985 bp Nichol, by permission of by Nichol and Black Moss Press.

Iroquois Lullaby: Collected by Alan Mills, Reprinted from *Canada's Story in Song* by Edith Fowke and Alan Mills.

PUFFIN BOOKS
Published by the Penguin Group
Penguin Books USA Inc., 375 Hudson Street, New York, New York 10014, U.S.A.
Penguin Books Ltd, 27 Wrights Lane, London W8 5TZ, England
Penguin Books Australia Ltd, Ringwood, Victoria, Australia
Penguin Books Canada Ltd, 10 Alcorn Avenue, Toronto, Ontario, Canada M4V 3B2
Penguin Books (N.Z.) Ltd, 182–190 Wairau Road, Auckland 10, New Zealand

Penguin Books Ltd, Registered Offices: Harmondsworth, Middlesex, England

First published in Canada by Kids Can Press Ltd., 1991
First published in the United States of America by Puffin Books,
a division of Penguin Books USA Inc., 1993

1 3 5 7 9 10 8 6 4 2

Anthology copyright © Houghton Mifflin Canada Limited, 1991
Illustrations copyright © Michael Martchenko, 1991
All rights reserved

LIBRARY OF CONGRESS CATALOGING-IN-PUBLICATION DATA
Zoomerang a boomerang: poems to make your belly laugh / compiled by
Caroline Parry; illustrated by Michael Martchenko.
—1st American ed.   p. cm.
Summary: A collection of humorous poems covering such topics as
pies, boomerangs, and polar bear golfers.
ISBN 0-14-054869-6
1. Children's poetry.   2. Humorous poetry.   [1. Poetry—
Collections.   2. Humorous poetry.]   I. Parry, Caroline.
II. Martchenko, Michael, ill.
PN6109.97Z66 1993   808.81'0083—dc20   92-26589

The first trade edition of *Zoomerang a Boomerang* was published in Canada by Kids
Can Press Ltd., and it was based on the Big Book, *A Rhyme for Me*,
published by Houghton Mifflin Canada Limited.

Printed in Mexico
Set in Optima

Contents

"Hello, Hello"

BY EVE MERRIAM

Hello, hello,
who's calling, please?
Mr. Macaroni
and a piece of cheese.

Hello, hello,
hello, who's there?
Honey Buzzbee
and a big brown bear.

Hello, hello,
will you spell your name?
It's R.A.T.
and yours is the same.

Hello, hello,
what did you say?
The rain is over,
let's go out and play.

Zoomerang a Boomerang

BY RUTH I. DOWELL

Zoomerang a boomerang
Around a maple tree!
Zoomerang a boomerang
But don't hit me!

Skyscraper

BY DENNIS LEE

Skyscraper, skyscraper,
Scrape me some sky:
Tickle the sun
While the stars go by.

Tickle the stars
While the sun's
climbing high,
Then skyscraper,
skyscraper,
Scrape me some sky.

Garbage Day

BY SHEREE FITCH

Smash the trash!
Smush it into mush!
Put it on the sidewalk
For the garbage truck.

Watch the men
Throw the bags in the back
Then the trap door closes
And the garbage gets
CRUSHED!

Oh My, No More Pie

BY ELLA JENKINS

Oh My,

No more pie.

Oh My,

No more pie.

Pie too sweet, think I'll have some meat.

Meat too red, think I'll have some bread.

Bread too brown, I better go to town.

Town too far, I think I'll drive the car.

Car too slow, I fell and stubbed my toe.

Toe gives me pain, I better take the train.

Train had a wreck, I almost broke my neck.

Oh My,

No more pie.

Oh My,

No more pie.

Everything Grows

BY RAFFI AND D. PIKE

Chorus

Everything grows and grows

Babies do, animals too

Everything grows

Everything grows and grows

Sisters do, brothers too

Everything grows

A blade of grass, fingers and toes

Hair on my head, a red, red, rose

Everything grows, anyone knows

That's how it goes

Chorus

Food on the farm, fish in the sea

Birds in the air, leaves on the tree

Everything grows, anyone knows

That's how it goes

Chorus

That's how it goes, under the sun

That's how it goes, under the rain

Everything grows, anyone knows

That's how it goes

Chorus

Jamboree

BY DAVID MCCORD

A rhyme for ham? *Jam.*

A rhyme for mustard? *Custard.*

A rhyme for steak? *Cake.*

A rhyme for rice? *Another slice.*

A rhyme for stew? *You.*

A rhyme for mush? *Hush!*

A rhyme for prunes? *Goons.*

A rhyme for pie? *I.*

A rhyme for iced tea? *Me.*

For the pantry shelf? *Myself.*

another poem

by sean o huigin

i count my

fingers

every one

and then my

feet when

i am

done

i count my

eyes

i count

my nose

i clap my

hands

and touch

my toes

i put my
head
down
close my
eyes
i try
to think
of butterflies

i listen
then
i raise
my head
and point
to something
that is
red

17

Hello, Sir

BY CAROLINE PARRY

Hello, sir.

Hello, sir.

Are you going to golf, sir?

No, sir.

Why, sir?

Because I've got a cold, sir.

Where did you get the cold, sir?

Up at the North Pole, sir.

What were you doing there, sir?

Catching polar bears, sir.

How many did you catch, sir?

1, sir, 2, sir, 3, sir,

4, sir, 5, sir, 6, sir,

7, sir, 8, sir, 9, sir,

10, sir —that's all I got, sir!

Aaatchoo!

Miss Polly Had a Dolly

TRADITIONAL

Miss Polly had a dolly who was

sick, sick, sick,

So she called for the doctor to come

quick, quick, quick.

The doctor came with his bag and his hat,

And he rapped on the door with a rat tat tat.

He looked at the dolly and shook his head,

And he said, "Miss Polly, put her straight
to bed."

He wrote on some paper for a pill, pill, pill.

"I'll be back in the morning with the
bill, bill, bill."

Head and Shoulders

TRADITIONAL

Head and shoulders, knees and toes,
Knees and toes, knees and toes.
Head and shoulders, knees and toes,
Eyes, ears, mouth and nose.

Tête, épaules, genoux et pieds,
Genoux et pieds, genoux et pieds.
Tête, épaules, genoux et pieds,
Les yeux, les oreilles, la bouche, le nez.

Tooth Day

BY BEATRICE SCHENK DE REGNIERS

Look! There is *nothing* to see.

The truth is a tooth used to be

Right here   when I smile.

Now we'll all wait a while

For the new tooth that's coming to me.

What Do You Suppose?

TRADITIONAL

What do you suppose?

A bee sat on my nose.

Then what do you think?

He gave me a wink

And said, "I beg your pardon,

I thought you were the garden."

Winter Signs

BY JACK PRELUTSKY

Winter signs are everywhere,
the winter winds are nipping,
winter snow is in my hair,
my winter nose is dripping.

Everywhere

by bp Nichol

Everywhere the fishes go

your wishes go your wishes go

everywhere the fishes go

your wishes go there too

Everywhere the birds can fly
your words can fly your words can fly
everywhere the birds can fly
your words can fly there too

Kookaburra

TRADITIONAL

Kookaburra sits on the old gum tree,
Merry merry king of the bush is he.
Laugh, Kookaburra!
Laugh, Kookaburra!
Gay your life must be!

Kookaburra sits on the old fence rail,
Picking the splinters out of his tail.
Cry, Kookaburra!
Cry, Kookaburra!
Sad your life must be!

Kookaburra sits on the old gum tree,

Eating all the gum drops he can see.

Stop, Kookaburra!

Stop, Kookaburra!

Save some drops for me!

What They Said

TRADITIONAL

Let's wake up,
Said the pup.

It's still dark,
Said the lark.

What's that?
Said the cat.

I want to sleep,
Said the sheep.

A bad habit,
Said the rabbit.

Of course,
Said the horse.

Let's have a spree,
Said the bee.

But where?
Said the hare.

In the barrow,
Said the sparrow.

I'm too big,
Said the pig.

In the house,
Said the mouse.

But the dog said — Bow-wow,
It's too late now.

31

Iroquois Lullaby

TRADITIONAL

Ho, Ho, Watanay,

Ho, Ho, Watanay,

Ho, Ho, Watanay,

Kiyokena, Kiyokena.

Do, do, mon petit,

Do, do, mon petit,

Do, do, mon petit

et bonne nuit, et bonne nuit.

Slumber, my little one,

Slumber, my little one,

Slumber, my little one

and gently sleep, so gently sleep.